# Juan Bobo
## Goes Up and Down the Hill

A Puerto Rican Folk Tale

Retold by Marisa Montes

Illustrated by Maurie J. Manning

HAMPTON-BROWN

# Characters

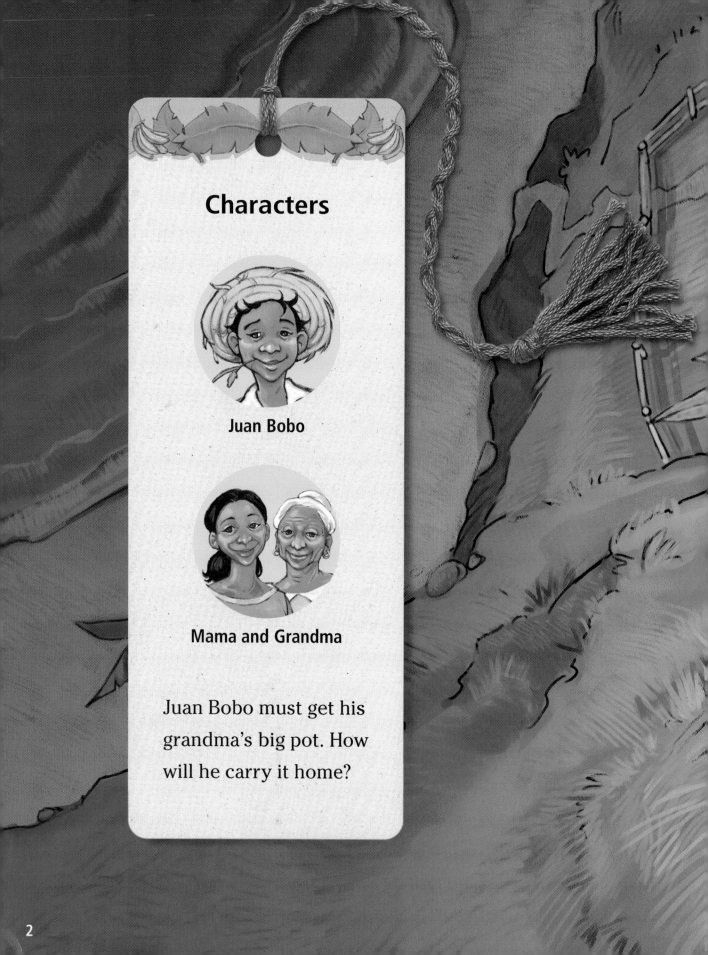

**Juan Bobo**

**Mama and Grandma**

Juan Bobo must get his grandma's big pot. How will he carry it home?

# Juan Bobo
## Goes Up and Down the Hill

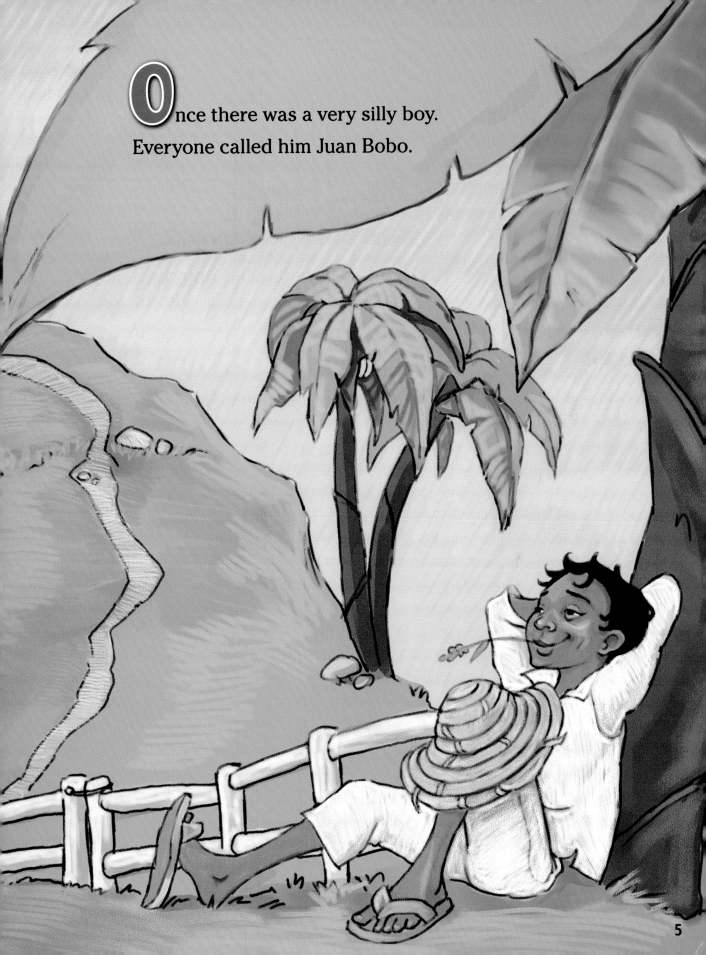

Once there was a very silly boy.
Everyone called him Juan Bobo.

One day, Juan Bobo's mother wanted to make soup. She had too many vegetables. They did not fit in her pot.

"Juan," Mama called, "go up the hill to your grandma's house. Borrow her big pot. It's the one with three legs."

# The Black Pot

In Grandmother's house,
way up on the hill,
In one of the cupboards,
on one of the shelves,
There's a shiny black pot
with three little legs.
That's where it should be.
Please bring it to me!

Juan groaned. He did not want to get the pot. He wanted to take a nap under the banana tree.

But he climbed up the hill to his grandmother's house.

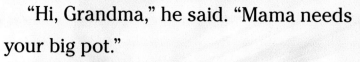

"Hi, Grandma," he said. "Mama needs your big pot."

"Which pot?" Grandma asked. She was standing in front of a cupboard.

Juan looked inside the cupboard. There were many dishes and pots on the shelves. Then he saw the black pot. "It's the one with three legs," he said.

# There's the Pot!

Juan stood next to the cupboard,
  in front of the red chair.
Juan saw the big, black pot,
  and he shouted, "It's right there!"

It's there below the dishes,
  there between the cups,
There above a big bowl
  full of coconuts.

Juan Bobo took the pot off the shelf
and carried it out the door. "It's heavy!"
he said.

"Juan," said his grandmother, "just take
it to your mama."

First, Juan Bobo carried the pot on his back. But his back hurt.

Then, he dragged the pot behind him. But it got caught on the rocks in the path!

Finally, he looked at the pot. "You have three legs, but I have two," he said. "Why am I carrying YOU, you lazy old thing?"

"Let's race down the hill to my house!"
Juan Bobo said to the pot. "I bet you can
run fast with three legs."

He stood next to the pot and yelled,
"One, two, three—GO!"

Juan Bobo raced down the
hill. As he ran, he sang.

# ♪ The Race

Jump over rocks,

Run down the hill,

And then go through
the gate.

Run up the steps,

Across the yard—

Oh, hurry, please
don't wait!

Juan Bobo raced into the house. He fell on the floor. He was so tired!

"Juan," Mama said, "where is the big pot?"

"Isn't it here yet?" Juan cried.

"What do you mean?" Mama said.

"I raced the pot down the hill," Juan Bobo said. "I have two legs, but it has three. Didn't it get here before me?"

"*Ay, ay, ay*, Juan!" Mama cried. "Go back up the hill! Get the pot, or someone will take it!"

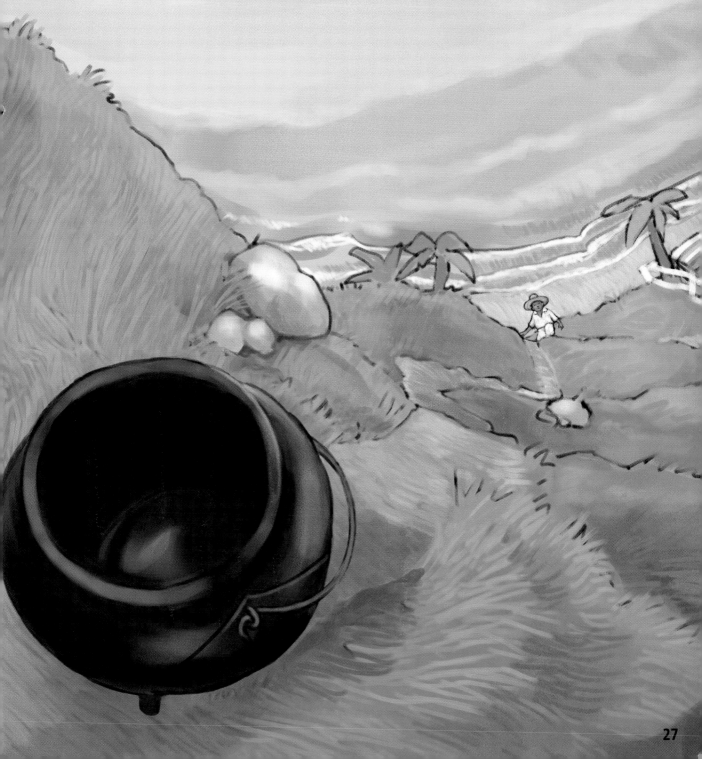

Poor Juan Bobo climbed up the
steep hill again.

The pot was still on the path.

"You lazy old thing!" Juan Bobo said. "You have three good legs, but you just sit there! You could race me if you tried."

Juan Bobo was mad. He kicked the pot hard.

BONG!

It began to roll down the hill.

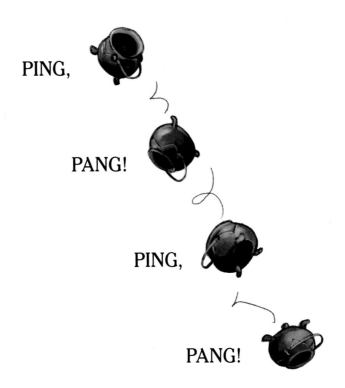

PING,

PANG!

PING,

PANG!

"Wait, you silly old pot!" Juan Bobo yelled.
"I haven't counted to three yet!" He ran after
the pot.

The pot didn't stop. It rolled down the hill, over the rocks, and through the gate. It bounced up the steps and across the yard. Then it went right into the kitchen.

Juan ran as fast as he could, but the pot won the race!

Juan Bobo didn't care. "I am so tired!" he said. "I am going to take a nap under the banana tree."

Then he fell asleep and dreamed of Mama's delicious soup!